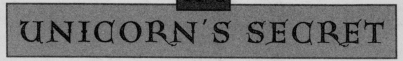

#8

The Journey Home

by Kathleen Duey
illustrated by Omar Rayyan

ALADDIN PAPERBACKS

New York   London   Toronto   Sydney   Singapore

For all the daydreamers . . .

First Aladdin Paperbacks edition December 2003

Text copyright © 2003 by Kathleen Duey
Illustrations copyright © 2003 by Omar Rayyan

A Ready-for-Chapters Book

ALADDIN PAPERBACKS
An imprint of Simon & Schuster
Children's Publishing Division
1230 Avenue of the Americas
New York, NY 10020

Also available in an Aladdin Library edition.
Designed by Debra Sfetsios
The text of this book was set in Golden Cockerel ITC.

Printed in the United States of America
2 4 6 8 10 9 7 5 3
ISBN 0-689-85374-2

The Library of Congress Control Number of the Library Edition is 2003111345

✦

Heart's camp is on a rocky ridge. She has decided to follow Lord Dunraven, convinced the old gardener he has taken prisoner knows something about the disappearance of the people of Castle Avamir—and about her parents. Moonsilver's tireless galloping has put them three days ahead. For once Heart doesn't have to hide or hurry. She reads Lord Irmaedith's storybook first. It's wonderful! But Lord Dunraven's book is different. . . .

✦

+CHAPTER ONE

Heart was frowning. She was so disappointed.

She had been hoping to read something about her family, about the unicorns—but so far Lord Dunraven's book was all about his castle. It talked about building the stone walls, the huge glass windows in the upstairs ballrooms, the towers. . . .

She looked up.

Moonsilver was grazing.

His white coat shone in the early sunlight.

She had taken off his armor.

They were safe here.

Behind her, to the east, the rocky wastelands stretched out for three days' journey—and beyond them were the steep slopes of Lord Levin's forests.

Heart squinted in the early sunlight, staring out

over the open land. That was the way they had come.

There were no roads in the wastelands.

The ground was crisscrossed with deep ravines. The rocks were as jagged as wolves' teeth.

No one ever traveled that way.

But Moonsilver had galloped over the broken ground for three days and nights.

He had leaped the gullies and the rocks.

By the time he had finally stopped, Heart had been stiff and sore.

Moonsilver hadn't seemed tired.

She had been exhausted.

She yawned, set the book aside, and stood up to stretch.

Before her the ridge cast a deep shadow westward.

Beyond that the early sun streaked the sloping land. It leveled out in the distance, along the Blue River.

She could see Ruth Oakes's house from where she stood.

It looked so small. River Road was visible. Crooked Lane wasn't, but Ruth's house stood on the corner and Heart knew exactly where the weed-lined little track ran.

Simon's shack was a long way down it, close to the Blue River. She couldn't see it, but she could picture it perfectly.

The thatched roof sagged; the leaning walls were the color of dirt. Inside, it was dark and dusty.

Heart blinked back tears, then traced the River Road with her eyes.

"Your mother and I walked that road almost every day," she told Moonsilver, "before you were born."

She wiped her eyes with her sleeve. She missed Avamir—and Kip.

Both of them were with the Gypsies, a week or more ahead of them, traveling their usual route toward Derrytown, then beyond.

At least she knew they were safe.

Binney loved them both.

Heart took a deep breath. She didn't have to

worry as much now. Moonsilver wasn't a spindly colt any longer.

He was tall and strong.

He could outdistance any lord's guardsmen and live happily grazing in meadows and drinking from creeks.

Heart would do her best to protect him, but it went both ways now. He would try to keep her safe too.

Heart sat back down.

She opened the book again and turned pages without reading them.

There were drawings of the high outer walls.

She studied a drawing of one of the towers. It had thin slits cut into the stone, but no windows.

There were drawings of the parapets, where the guards would stand, keeping watch.

The next few pages looked like a jumble of squares and rectangles at first, then Heart read the tiny print that labeled each room.

The guards' quarters were on the lowest floor, in the center of the castle.

The floors above had guest rooms and ballrooms and huge banquet halls.

Heart turned the pages until she spotted the design of the two rearing unicorns.

The same design was on her baby blanket—the one Simon had sold, the one Lord Dunraven had in a trunk in his castle.

For the thousandth time Heart wondered where her parents were and why they had left her beside the Blue River.

Maybe they were among the people of Castle Avamir.

It seemed likely from all she had learned.

But where had they gone?

Heart stared at the book without seeing the page. Lord Dunraven was a powerful and terrible man. She would have to find a way to talk with the old gardener, to ask him where the people were now.

Heart's eyes focused on the print below the drawing.

Zim had once tried to sound out the letters for her.

Now she could read the words by herself.

"'Beyond these iron gates, at the end of the Old Road, lie The Mountains of the Moon,'" Heart read aloud, clearly and carefully. "'Ancient tales say unicorns once lived there. This is quite true.'"

She took a quick breath, surprised.

The road to the Mountains of the Moon was near Dunraven's Castle?

Was it the Old Road Binney had talked about?

Heart looked up from the book, remembering. Binney had said no one could travel that way, now that Lord Dunraven had closed it. With the Sunset Gates? Were they the iron gates Joseph Lequire's ancestor had made?

Moonsilver lifted his head from the fresh grass.

"Do you know where The Mountains of the Moon are?" she asked him.

He struck at the ground with a forehoof.

He shook his mane.

Heart wished as always that she could just *talk* to him.

"Are there other unicorns? Is that where they are?" Heart whispered.

Moonsilver pawed at the ground again, flinging tufts of grass backward. The disappearance of the unicorns, Lord Dunraven's destroying old story-books, forbidding common folks to learn to read, her family . . . these things were all tied together somehow, Heart was sure.

She had to figure out *how*.

Heart felt the silver bracelet on her wrist tighten. She pushed up her sleeve.

The bracelet looked like fancy silver lace, with a tiny silver flower in the center.

Heart touched it.

The gardener at Castle Avamir had given her a real flower. What magic had changed it into this tiny metal one?

Moonsilver switched his tail and tossed his head, turning to face the River Road.

Heart heard the distant hoofbeats a moment later.

There they were, riding at a gallop.

Lord Dunraven rode a little way ahead of his men.

His white hair had escaped his hood.

His dark cloak fanned out behind him.

One of the horses still labored under the weight of two men. The old man from Castle Avamir rode awkwardly, slumped against the guardsman's back.

Heart frowned.

The gardener had seemed very old.

He had to be exhausted.

Lord Dunraven had said something about a queen wanting to see the old man. Was there a queen among Castle Avamir's people?

There were kings and queens in the storybook Lord Irmaedith had given her.

Maybe somewhere there was a king's castle.

Heart smiled. The idea delighted her.

Then she frowned again.

Would a real king be wise and kind like the one in the storybook—or would he be like Lord Dunraven, but even more powerful?

Heart wished she had asked the young Lord Irmaedith for more storybooks. He had lots of them, she was sure. He loved books, and he could have anything he wanted.

He was the newly named Lord Irmaedith, ruler of lands even wider than Lord Dunraven's.

Heart wondered if she would ever see him again. He had told her his real name. "Seth." She said it aloud, hoping he was well.

Heart turned to Moonsilver.

"Eat your fill," she told him. "We'll follow them later tonight."

Heart played her flute for a time, quietly, letting the notes blend into the evening breeze.

While there was still a little light, she practiced writing. Her letters were getting neater.

She read until sunset. She slept lightly for a few hours, then rose and packed her carry-sack by starlight.

She was careful with Lord Dunraven's book.

She was no thief.

She would return the book to him very soon—one way or another.

+CHAPTER TWO

Heart started off, following the ridge for a long way, then dropping down to the River Road.

Moonsilver kept trotting ahead.

Heart thought about trying to put the braided halter and the lead rope on him.

Then she decided not to.

It felt wrong. And a lead rope could tangle in his legs if they were chased.

"Don't forget," she called after him. "You have to walk close by me in Ash Grove."

Moonsilver tossed his head.

He slowed a little.

Heart caught up. She glanced at Moonsilver. "Do you remember Ruth?"

He switched his tail back and forth.

Heart sighed. "She saved your life. You must remember her."

Moonsilver touched her cheek. His muzzle was soft as new moss. Heart looked into his dark eyes.

He could understand her, she was sure. She only wished she could understand him half as well.

Heart walked a little faster.

It was still dark when they rounded the last long bend.

There was no light shining from Ruth's windows.

Her whole house was dark.

Ruth was often up this early and Heart had been hoping to see a lantern lit. But she wasn't worried.

"She's off taking care of someone," Heart told Moonsilver. "Or sleeping."

Moonsilver walked lightly, in his graceful, quiet way.

They followed the path to the door.

Heart knocked gently.

There was no answer.

Heart stilled her own breath to listen, hoping to hear some tiny sound from inside the house.

But there was none.

She knocked again, louder.

But Ruth was not at home.

Heart turned away sadly. She glanced down Crooked Lane as they left. Simon's shack was down toward the river. She hoped he was well, that he had enough to eat, but she had no wish to see him.

Heart started toward Ash Grove.

It gave her comfort to know that the Gypsies—and Avamir and Kip—had probably passed this way a few weeks before.

Of course they never stopped in Ash Grove.

Lord Dunraven had a man in each town.

In Ash Grove that man was Tin Blackaby. He ran the town harshly. No one in Ash Grove had enough money to pay for a Gypsy show.

Heart shivered. She was uneasy.

Twice before she'd barely escaped from Ash Grove.

She could feel her pulse quicken as they turned onto Crosswater Street.

They crossed the Tirin Creek bridge. No one cried out. If guardsmen were around, none of them spotted a girl and an armored white stallion walking close together in the darkness.

The moon was rising.

Heart walked faster.

The houses seemed so small to her now.

She noticed loose shutters. The moonlight silvered the outlines of sagging roofs.

Had it always been like this?

It looked so . . . poor, so sad.

Heart passed Trader's Path, then Market Street, and then she could hear the river ahead in the darkness.

Heart reached up to lay one hand on Moonsilver's cheek.

From a distance it would look like she was holding a halter rope.

If Lord Dunraven had men watching the road, they would be here, guarding the Blue River Bridge.

She straightened her shoulders.

No stable page would hunch like a rabbit creeping past a hound yard.

Noble children—even the ones poor enough to work taking care of fancy horses—were not afraid of crossing a bridge, day or night.

They grew up in castles and cities.

They always had enough to eat.

They had warm beds and good boots and clear-glass lanterns.

They had *books*.

Heart lifted her chin. She could read as well as or better than any noble child now. She refused to look behind herself again.

Every muscle in her body tense, she stepped onto the planks of the bridge. "Stay close," she whispered to Moonsilver.

The river rushed past below them.

Moonsilver tossed his head.

Heart twined her fingers into his mane to keep him beside her as they crossed. She listened for shouts, for hoofbeats, but the night was silent. Finally they walked off the planks.

Heart walked fast, following the Derrytown road. The people of Castle Avamir were her family, she was almost sure. They had disappeared and she believed Lord Dunraven had something to do with it.

She had to find a way to help them.

+CHAPTER THREE

Heart's muscles were as hard as hickory wood from all her traveling, but Lord Dunraven and his men were mounted.

She couldn't keep up on foot.

The second morning, Moonsilver knelt and Heart climbed onto his back. He galloped through the forests.

He leaped fallen trees and boulders.

Heart was a steady rider now.

She sat, balanced, following his movements perfectly.

"There they are," Heart told Moonsilver whenever she spotted Lord Dunraven and his men through the trees.

Every time, he slowed to a trot, his hoofbeats light and quiet.

They had to stay out of sight.

Each evening Heart made small, careful cook-fires.

She was running out of barley; she boiled only a little.

She finished Lord Dunraven's book on the third night.

It was amazing. The castle was like a small city within high walls.

The builders had put two secret doors in the massive stone walls. She already knew about one of them—she was planning on using it.

As the days passed, Heart began to read Lord Irmaedith's storybook again every evening before she slept.

The tales were like old friends by now.

In many of them the unicorns healed people.

Heart knew that much was true. She had seen Moonsilver heal people—twice.

As it got dusky on the sixth night, Moonsilver lay down in the soft grass.

Heart spread her blanket.

For a long time she lay staring at the stars.

When she fell asleep, she dreamed she was running in moon-colored mountains. It was a familiar dream.

But this time she didn't feel like she was being chased.

She felt like she was running *toward* something.

The next morning Heart noticed a fine carriage on the road. A few hours later she caught a glimpse of a whole party of noblemen, the silver on their saddles flashing in the sunlight.

The morning after that Heart left Moonsilver grazing in a safe meadow and went into Derrytown alone.

She was nearly out of food.

She played her flute in the street and collected coins for supper. It took longer than usual.

"The Gypsies were here a few days past," an old man apologized. "Gave them all my coppers."

Heart lowered the flute and watched him walk away.

Binney and the Gypsies must have traveled

slowly. Heart smiled. Maybe she could catch up with them.

The next morning Heart guided Moonsilver straight through the woods instead of following the wide curves of the road. "There it is," she whispered at the first glimpse of the great stone walls.

Moonsilver danced to a halt, tossing his head.

Heart slid to the ground and stood beside him.

She heard hoofbeats.

She watched through the trees. Lord Dunraven spurred his tired horse into a gallop.

His men followed.

A trumpet sounded from somewhere on top of the castle walls.

Lord Dunraven's guards had spotted him. The trumpets were announcing his arrival.

"There's a door in the side wall," Heart told Moonsilver. "You can't see it from here."

Moonsilver looked at her.

Heart laid her hand on his neck.

Below, Lord Dunraven shouted a command.

The castle gates opened.

The guards bowed as Lord Dunraven galloped past.

The guards let their weary horses drop back to a trot.

Heart saw the old man slide sideways. The guardsman reached back to drag him upright.

The heavy gates swung shut with a creaking groan that echoed across the valley.

Heart took a deep breath. There were so many guards!

She was scared.

✦CHAPTER FOUR

As the stars glittered overhead, Heart heard the gates swing open four more times. She heard shouted greetings and laughter.

Noblemen and women were coming to Dunraven's castle.

Maybe Lord Dunraven's guards would be too busy with guests to notice her.

She forced herself to sleep, dozing uneasily as she waited.

Finally, in the middle of the night, Heart woke Moonsilver.

"I have to go alone," she said quietly. Moonsilver shook his mane and stamped a forehoof.

Heart reached up.

He lowered his head, pushing his muzzle gently against the center of her chest.

His horn rested on her left shoulder.

It felt cold as creek water, as it always did.

Her eyes filled with tears.

"I'll try to be back in an hour or two," she said. "But don't worry if it takes longer. Just wait for me unless someone comes too near."

She clasped her arms tightly around his neck and closed her eyes.

She kissed his silk-white cheek.

Then she stepped back.

She started to put his armor on, but he shied away from her.

Heart faced him. "But if things go wrong and you have to go find Binney and your mother without me, the armor will help you hide."

Moonsilver backed away, pawing at the ground.

Heart gave in; the decision was his to make.

She stacked the armor carefully in a narrow place between two boulders the size of cottages.

Scrambling back out, she memorized the shape of the rocks.

She had to be able to find them when she returned.

Moonsilver was watching her.

Heart picked up her carry-sack. "If danger comes close, follow the road out of Derrytown to find the Gypsies. Your mother and Binney will know what to do."

Heart kissed his muzzle lightly, then turned and walked away before she started crying.

The night was silent except for the velvet rush of an owl's wings overhead and the sound of her footsteps.

Heart glanced back.

Moonsilver looked strange and magical in the near dark.

Heart turned and lengthened her steps.

She had no time to waste.

She could feel the hard edges of Lord Dunraven's book against her back.

She would leave it exactly where she had found it. The little room held so many amazing things. . . .

The sound of voices scattered Heart's thoughts.

People arriving this late?

She could just make out the last curve in the

road before it passed through the castle gates.

There were hoofbeats mixed with footsteps.

A shout from the travelers brought an answer from the castle wall.

Perfect. The guards would be busy; the sound of the gates creaking open would cover her footfalls. . . .

Heart hesitated only an instant. Then she began to run.

✦CHAPTER FIVE

Heart was careful to stay in the cover of the trees.

She had been here once, following Simon. The guardsmen had opened the little door that night. The light shining from within had guided her to it.

Now she would have to find it herself.

Peering through the trees, she came to an uncertain stop.

The door was narrow.

She remembered that much clearly.

And it had a rounded top.

Heart stared at the long wall of gray stone. There were high windows, spilling golden light. One of the ballrooms?

A sudden sound of laughter sifted downward through the still air.

Heart tensed, listening.

Music began, a lively tune. There were flutes and pipes. There were other instruments she had never heard before.

Lord Dunraven was entertaining guests at this hour?

Heart exhaled.

She had thought the castle would be quiet and still.

She glanced at the sky.

She had a few hours before dawn, and not a second to waste.

Heart sprinted across the clearing, sliding to a halt beside the castle wall. There were no shouts. No one had seen her.

Heart began to work her way along the wall, her fingers brushing the stone.

It was smooth as river rock, worn by rain and wind.

Heart bit her lip. The wall went on and on; the castle was enormous. What if she couldn't find the door?

She began to count her steps, trying not to panic.

Finally, on step 217, she felt something.

She rubbed her hands across the stone again.

It was a crack, narrow and long, running straight upward from the ground.

Heart traced it as high as she could reach.

There. She touched the tiny notch in the stone.

Instantly there was a soft scraping sound as the door swung open.

Heart darted inside.

The hallway was dark as moonless midnight.

But Heart remembered: It ran straight and wide for a long way.

Every muscle in her body tight with fear, she began to walk forward. There were open arches of stone on both sides of her, she knew. But she couldn't see them now.

The empty air beneath her fingers told her when she came to the first wide arch.

She passed it, then three more, then she

stopped. She wasn't sure; she hadn't counted on that long-ago night.

Heart crossed her legs and sat on the hard, cool stone.

She opened her carry-sack and felt for her candle stub.

Her fire striker and tinder were in a little box.

She didn't need to see. Her hands had done this chore thousands of times.

In an eye's blink she had one of the candles lit.

The flickering, amber light flowed up the walls, making soft-edged shadows.

Heart picked up her carry-sack, holding the candle out in front of her.

This room was the one she remembered!

Heart stared at the table.

It was carved from heavy, dark wood—its legs were shaped like rearing unicorns, perfectly lifelike.

The flickering candle made it seem as though they were breathing.

Heart turned to the trunk against the wall. She lifted the heavy lid.

There it was. . . .

The bracelet on her arm tightened gently. Heart took a slow deep breath before she touched her baby blanket.

For a moment she stared at the silver thread sparkling in the candlelight.

Then she folded the blanket carefully and slipped it into her carry-sack.

She turned to the cabinet.

There, on a low shelf, she saw the carving of a unicorn horn.

She had wanted to touch it last time she had been in this odd little room, but there had been no time.

She stared at it.

Moonsilver's horn was silvery.

This one was dark oak wood.

Heart opened the glass doors to the cabinet.

The bracelet on her arm tightened the instant she reached out. The horn was far too light to be wood.

Heart took a quick breath. It was colder than the stone, almost icy.

Maybe it was real?

Thoughts chased each other through Heart's mind.

If it was true that the lords had long ago hunted unicorns . . .

Could this age-darkened horn be a terrible memento of that cruel long-ago time?

Heart wasn't a thief.

She had come to take her own blanket, and to return the book.

"But if the horn *is* real," she whispered to herself, "it doesn't belong to Lord Dunraven."

Heart took Lord Dunraven's book out of her carry-sack.

Then she rolled all her precious things up inside the blanket: her flute, her quill and paper, her storybook, and the unicorn horn.

She rolled it tightly, wrapping the plain edge around as far as she could to hide the silver embroidery.

Then she wrapped her tattered sleeping blanket around the bundle.

She tied it up with twine and slipped it into her carry-sack.

Heart exhaled slowly. No matter what else happened this night, her baby blanket was hers again.

Heart picked up Lord Dunraven's book.

It was heavy.

She faced the shelves, trying to remember which one it had been on. She couldn't. Finally she just reached up to slide it into place.

There were so many books! Heart longed to read them all.

The sound of heavy boots on the stone floor startled her.

"What do you think you are doing?" a rasping voice demanded from behind her.

A cold ball of fear settled in Heart's stomach.

Lord Dunraven!

✦CHAPTER SIX

"Turn around," Lord Dunraven said.

Heart swallowed hard. Her legs felt weak.

She slid the book onto the shelf, took a deep, shaky breath, and turned.

Lord Dunraven's face was dark with anger.

A guardsman stood behind him, holding a torch.

"You aren't one of my pages," Lord Dunraven began, then he narrowed his eyes. "I remember you," he said slowly. "You were in the stall with the white mare in Bidenfast. What Lord do you serve?"

Heart's legs ached to run.

"Where is that young stallion with the horn-spike armor?" he asked, leaning down to look into her face. Then he noticed her carry-sack. "What's in that?"

"There's nothing of yours," Heart said quickly. She met Lord Dunraven's eyes. It was true. The blanket was rightfully hers. The unicorn horn did not belong to him either.

"Look in it," Lord Dunraven commanded the guardsman.

Heart could hear her blood pounding inside her veins.

She tried to step backward, but the guardsman jerked her carry-sack from her hands.

He pushed her bundled blanket back and forth, staring into the bottom of the cloth bag.

He finally looked up. "Nothing. Barley, some apples, a ball of twine, a candle stub, and an old blanket."

Heart lowered her eyes.

She waited for the guard to say more, but he didn't.

He hadn't felt her book or the horn through the thick wool of the blankets.

"Why have you come here?" Lord Dunraven demanded. Then he laughed. "It hardly matters. In an hour the hunt will begin. If you left that stallion somewhere in the woods, we'll find him eventually."

Heart couldn't help glancing up at him.

He scowled at her. "The young lord got well after you met him."

Heart blinked.

"It happened very quickly, almost like magic," he added, then he paused as though she was supposed to say something. She lowered her eyes. "Take her to the tower," he ordered. "She can stay there until after the hunt."

"Yes, m'lord," the guard answered.

Lord Dunraven walked away. Once his footsteps had faded to silence, the guard snuffed out Heart's candle and handed it to her.

He let her pick up her carry-sack, then turned her around and pushed her forward.

Heart walked slowly.

She shuffled her feet on the smooth stone, trying to think.

It would be hard for her to outrun the guard in the dark.

"Walk faster," the guard said, nudging her shoulder.

Heart took slightly longer steps.

The hallway with the arches met a much wider corridor. It was like a town road, wide enough for twenty men to walk shoulder-to-shoulder.

Torches were set high on the walls, far enough apart that deep shadows gathered between them.

The guard guided her straight down the center of the corridor. After a time he gripped her shoulder and pulled again, this time to the right.

They walked a long way, making two more turns.

Heart was getting desperate. She had to get away soon or . . .

"Up the stairs," the guard said.

Startled, Heart lifted her head.

The guard gestured to the right and she stared.

She had never seen a staircase like this one.

The steps curved, spiraling tightly like a snail's shell.

There were torches on the walls.

She could not see the top of the steps, but she knew this had to be one of the towers.

The guardsman pushed her forward.

Heart hoisted her carry-sack higher on her shoulder.

Then she began to climb slowly, her knees stiff with fear.

Halfway up, her legs aching, she stumbled. The guardsman reached out to steady her and she glanced back.

His eyes met hers for an instant.

He looked sad, then angry. Heart climbed upward again.

"There's your room," the guard said when they finally topped the last step. Heart saw six doors, three on each side of a narrow hall. They were heavy, hewn from dark wood. The hinges and clasps were thick bronze.

"That one," the guardsman said impatiently, pointing.

Heart took a single step toward the first door on the left.

The bracelet on her wrist tightened painfully for an instant.

Heart hesitated. Why now? Why hadn't it warned her before Lord Dunraven had come up behind her?

The guardsman nudged her forward. He was reaching around her, turning a long brass key, then lifting the iron hasp that held the door shut.

Heart shivered.

She tried to turn, but he grabbed her shoulders and pushed her forward. Heart stumbled inside.

She whirled around, but the guard was closing the door behind her.

Heart stood in the dark, trembling, listening to the heavy footsteps fade as he went down the steep stairs.

Heart clenched her fists, furious with herself for getting caught, for not even trying to run.

She would stand by the door.

When it opened again, she would push past the guard. She would run and—

Heart heard rustling sounds in the darkness.

She gripped her carry-sack and braced herself.

"Who is there?" she asked in the steadiest voice she could manage.

"I am, child."

Heart very nearly fell to her knees.

The voice was familiar to her ears, to her heart. She stared at the vague shape of a woman in the darkness.

"Ruth?" she whispered. "Ruth Oakes?"

✦CHAPTER SEVEN

Heart felt Ruth's arms circle her shoulders.

For a long moment Heart leaned against her, inhaling the familiar smell of herbs and soap.

Then she stepped back.

"I have a candle," she told Ruth.

"Good," Ruth said gently, and Heart could imagine her smiling.

A second later she felt Ruth's hand on her shoulder and the warmth of Ruth's breath on her cheek. "Are Avamir and Moonsilver all right?" she breathed. "Just nod. Don't speak until you light the candle."

Heart nodded, puzzled.

Then Ruth stood back.

Heart fumbled through her carry-sack. Her fingers finally closed on her tinderbox.

She took out her worn striker and managed a spark on the first try.

Once the candle was lit, Heart looked up, excited to see Ruth's much-loved face.

Instead she saw a ring of faces.

There were at least twenty people in the darkened room.

They were standing nearly shoulder-to-shoulder along the walls.

Heart held the candle higher.

They were dressed in fine clothes like lords and ladies.

She noticed an old man, leaning on the woman next to him.

He lifted his head to smile at her. Heart caught her breath. This was the old man from Castle Avamir. Then these people had to be—

"Heart," Ruth began, taking the candle to hold it higher. "Why are you here?"

"A little light to chase our fears! Now we will all want to explain ourselves, I think," the gardener said gently. He gestured toward Ruth.

"I am the healer from Ash Grove," she said. "Lord Dunraven sent for me in case anyone was hurt hunting. But then . . . the guards brought me here."

One of the men stepped forward. "Healer, we are honored to meet you. We were brought here from our castle by Dunraven's guards."

It was Heart's turn.

"Be careful," Ruth whispered. "Don't tell them everything."

But before Heart could answer, the old man seized her hand, raising her arm above her head.

Her sleeve fell to her elbow.

The room went so still it was as though every person there had stopped breathing.

The silver bracelet sparkled in the candlelight.

It looked like silver lace; the tiny silver flower in the center shone softly.

Ruth straightened. "Where did you get that?"

The old man sighed. There was joy on his tired face. "She got it bit by bit, I imagine."

Heart stared at him.

He was right.

The silver threads in the bracelet had been given to her by Binney and Ruth—and two had come from Simon; he had pulled them from the embroidery on her blanket before he sold it.

Heart hugged her carry-sack.

"Are any of you," she began, her throat tight, "are any of you my family?" Her voice cracked under the weight of her feelings.

The old man smiled. "Not me. But the others are *all* your family one way or another."

"Are my parents here?" Heart asked, her voice sinking to a whisper. She waited, listening to the silence that followed her question.

"That bracelet could belong only to the daughter of our queen," one woman said quietly.

Heart stared at her. "Your queen?"

"Yes," the woman answered. "Queen by deed, not birth. We have no nobility. I wish we knew where she was." She sighed. "And your brother, if he lives."

Heart stared.

She had a brother?

"Was he left for someone else to raise too?"

The woman shook her head sadly. "We just don't know."

Heart felt her eyes stinging.

"Where are the rest of the people from Castle Avamir?" she asked them, wiping at her eyes.

"We are all who are left," an old woman answered.

Ruth looked up sharply. "Avamir? That was my great-grandmother's name."

"Most healers are related to us one way or another," a woman interrupted her gently.

Ruth shook her head. "I'm probably not. My grandmother had no family—she was a foundling, like Heart. That why I gave Heart her name."

One of the women touched Ruth's cheek. "We have saved our children that way for generations—by making them someone else's children."

The bracelet tightened so hard that Heart flinched.

The gardener chuckled. "The magic wants you to pay attention."

Ruth turned. "Magic?"

Heart explained about the bracelet, how the silver threads had woven themselves into lace.

The people of Castle Avamir listened intently, smiling at one another.

Ruth shook her head. "That sounds like one of the old stories."

"Oh," the gardener said, "most of the old stories are true, more or less."

"So you all believe in unicorns?" Heart asked timidly.

"Of course!" a woman said. They all laughed.

"Heart!" Ruth touched her arm. "Tibbs left Derrytown, I was told."

Heart knew Ruth was changing the subject, reminding her to be careful, not to trust these strangers just yet.

Heart faced Ruth and smiled. "He asked me to tell you that he is very happy."

Ruth's eyes shone in the dim candlelight.

Heart nodded. "He's working with a master blacksmith named Joseph Lequire and—"

A murmur rose in the room and Heart glanced up. The people were staring at her.

"How do you know Joseph?" a man asked, leaning forward.

"I stayed at his forge," Heart said cautiously. How could she explain anything about Joseph without talking about the unicorns? An awkward moment passed. "A girl named Laura asked me to tell Terrin and Leah that she misses them," Heart said to cover her uneasiness.

A sound of surprise went through the room. Two girls stepped forward. "I'm Leah," one said. She gestured. "This is Terrin."

Heart smiled, glad to have diverted everyone's attention. "Laura was found in a vegetable patch when she was a babe," Heart said.

Terrin bit at her lip. "We should have known," she whispered to Leah.

Just then, the sound of a key turning in the door lock startled them all into silence.

✦CHAPTER EIGHT

Heart put out her candle and slipped it back into her carry-sack.

Without a word, she pulled Ruth toward the door, then pushed her gently against the wall.

A second later the door opened inward.

Heart and Ruth shrank back against the cold stone.

"Where's the old man?" the guard demanded. He held a lantern high to see into the little room.

The light angled inside, missing Heart and Ruth by a hand's breadth.

"Here," the gardener said. He stepped forward and the lantern light caught his face. "Could you give me your arm, sir? I am not strong."

The guard stepped into the little room, keeping

an eye on the people who stood against the back wall of the little room.

In that instant Ruth nudged Heart sideways, out the door.

Heart ducked around the corner, her back pressed against the wall.

She heard Ruth cough and knew the guard would too. "Move away from that door!" he shouted.

"I am sorry," Ruth said politely, calmly.

The guard lowered his voice. "Stand closer to the others, please, ma'am."

"How long will I have to stay here?" Ruth asked, keeping her voice mild. "I am the healer from Ash Grove."

Heart clutched her carry-sack to her chest.

"And how long must we stay?" one of the women from Castle Avamir asked.

Then the people in the little room were all talking at once.

Heart knew they were hiding the sound of her footsteps, her breathing. She was grateful.

She slipped deeper into the shadows.

The guard's lantern made the doorway glow yellow-orange.

Heart tiptoed to the end of the corridor.

Standing in the dark, she watched the guard bring the gardener out.

He closed the heavy door. The brass key glinted in the lantern light.

Heart got a good look. The key was shaped like a tower.

The gardener was still talking. "What does Lord Dunraven want with me?" he demanded.

"You know why you are here," the guard said.

The old man shook his head. He didn't answer.

The guard lifted his lantern.

Heart watched them start down the steep steps.

She waited until their footsteps faded into silence. Then she stepped forward in the dark.

She traced the wall with her fingers, and at the last door she stopped.

"I will come back," she said quietly. "I'll find the keys."

"We will be waiting," Ruth said just as softly from inside the little room. "Be careful."

Heart pressed the palm of her hand against the door.

Then she went to the top of the stairs.

The torchlight made her blink as she looked down.

The gardener was leaning on the guard's arm.

Heart waited until they were out of sight, then she started downward, staying close to the inside wall, her thoughts moving as fast as her feet.

Once they were all well away and safe in the forest, she had a hundred more questions to ask the people from Castle Avamir.

At the bottom of the steps, Heart darted into the shadows along the wall.

A long way up the corridor, the weary old man was hobbling along beside the young guard.

This passage was wide and the torches were far apart, mounted high on the walls.

Between them the shadows were thick.

Heart ran, light footed, darting beneath the torches.

Once she had caught up, she slowed and followed.

After a few minutes she noticed another guard walking toward them.

Heart crouched in a pool of shadows. Holding perfectly still, she waited.

This guard was tall and thin and his hair was graying. He was almost running. "Lord Dunraven should be back before too long," he called as he got closer.

The younger guard looked surprised. "Already?"

"They left long before sun up."

Heart held her breath.

"Young Lord Irmaedith wouldn't go," the guard said in a low voice as he got close.

The younger one nodded. "I heard."

"He's a fool to anger Lord Dunraven," the tall man said. He turned to the old man. "They want you kept upstairs—to wait for Lord Dunraven."

The old man stepped forward, frowning.

Yawning, the younger guard watched them walk away.

Heart waited, motionless and silent, staring at the key on his belt, thinking. The young Lord Irmaedith—Seth—was here?

She blushed, wondering if he would even recognize her.

Finally the young guard began to walk again.

Heart followed. She had studied the drawings in Lord Dunraven's book. The guards ate and slept down here somewhere, deep in the castle, far from fresh air or sunlight.

As they went, more and more guards walked up and down the corridor.

Heart pressed herself against the wall whenever they passed.

Every time, she was so scared, she trembled.

But the men were all talking. They joked with one another. They walked down the center of the massive hallway and none of them looked right or left.

Heart steadied herself. Her family was depending on her. Ruth was depending on her. Moonsilver was waiting for her.

She stood up and followed the young guard once the others had passed.

Finally he turned up a narrow corridor.

Heart peeked around the corner.

He was standing in front of a wall full of iron hooks.

He hung the key on one of the highest ones, then went on.

Heart watched until he turned up another corridor and disappeared.

Then she straightened up and squared her shoulders.

✦CHAPTER NINE

Heart listened.

The wide corridor was silent. She couldn't see anyone in either direction. Perfect. But she knew she had no time to waste.

Scared, her breath coming in quick little gasps, she set down her carry-sack.

All she needed was half a minute—maybe less.

She peeked around the corner once more. The smaller corridor was still empty. She knew it wouldn't be, not for long. The guards' quarters were up this way—men would be coming and going constantly.

Heart took a long breath, then sprinted up the passage, her eyes fixed on the iron key hooks.

She jumped and missed three times. They were higher than she had thought.

Frantic, her pulse pounding, she backed up a little way, then ran, leaping as high as she could.

Her fingers touched the key, then closed around it.

She dropped back to the stone, the key in her grasp. Then she whirled around and fled.

She slid around the corner into the wide corridor, and sank into the shadows along the wall. Her pulse was beating like bird wings in her throat.

An instant after she was hidden, a guard came into sight.

Heart watched him approach.

He turned down the narrow passage, passing so close that she could have touched him.

His footsteps faded to silence.

Still trembling, Heart forced herself to stand up, then run back toward the tower.

The steep staircase seemed twice as long this time.

Heart's legs ached and her breathing burned as she climbed.

Panting, she finally came to the top and staggered into the short corridor.

Her hands shaking, she pushed the key into the lock.

It fit perfectly.

The instant she opened the door, the people of Castle Avamir poured out.

"Follow me," Heart managed between breaths. Then she frowned. "Where's Ruth?"

One of the women touched Heart's cheek. "Two guards came for her."

The girl named Terrin nodded. "They said someone was hurt."

Heart's stomach tightened. She had wanted Ruth to come away with them. Lord Dunraven could not be trusted. "I know a way out," she said as she led the way down the stairs, "but you have to be quiet and stay close."

Heart was worried about the noise so many people would make. Minutes later, she turned around on the steep steps to make sure they were still behind her.

They were nearly silent.

In the wide corridor, the people of Castle Avamir spread out.

They formed two long, ragged lines, one on each side of the corridor.

Heart put her carry-sack over her shoulder and ran, sprinting past the torches, stopping in the shadows when guards came close.

No one fell behind.

The old people moved as swiftly as the children.

Heart followed the wide corridor for a long way, then made the first turn, then the second. They were close to the last turn when the sound of heavy boots brought them all to a stop.

"Hurry!" a guard was shouting from a side-passage up ahead. "They say he might not live!"

Everyone flattened against the walls. Heart turned her head, crouching, completely motionless, completely silent. Three guards ran past.

Heart hoped that Ruth could help whomever had been hurt. Heart knew she would do her best; she was a true healer.

Heart stood and started running again. The people of Castle Avamir followed her silently.

When they finally reached the long corridor with the arches, Heart paused.

There were no torches on the walls here. It was still dark as midnight all the way to the door at the end of the passageway.

"Join hands," she whispered, digging through her carry-sack.

She lit a candle stub.

Terrin took Heart's free hand and reached out toward Leah. In a moment they were all linked together.

Heart led the way, the candle casting just enough light to guide her.

At the round-topped door, she hesitated. "There could be guards outside," she whispered. "There weren't when I came in, but . . ."

Heart eased the door open just wide enough to peer out—and caught her breath.

The sky was just beginning to lighten, but there was a bonfire blazing high.

Torches had been fastened to long iron rods.

In the flickering orange-yellow light Heart could see the whole meadow: It was full of people.

+CHAPTER TEN

Heart jerked the door closed, breathlessly describing what she had seen.

"It's an entertainment," Terrin whispered. "Nobles have them all the time. Games, prizes—they'll have flower tea and pastries to eat."

Heart fought to stay calm. "I thought we could just run to the woods from here—that most the men would be out hunting with Lord Dunraven."

The people fell into a silence so deep it was as though they had disappeared in the darkness.

"Hunting?" an old man echoed after a long pause. "Up the Old Road?"

Heart hesitated, wondering for the first time what Lord Dunraven meant to hunt. Were there unicorns left in The Mountains of the Moon? Her mouth went dry.

"We must leave this place now," a woman whispered.

Heart pushed the door open again and pressed her eye against the little crack.

It looked like a town fair, in a way, except that the people all wore fine clothes.

She saw noblewomen using sticks to hit a wooden ball.

Children wearing silk coats ran in circles, laughing.

People stood near the bonfire, warming their hands. Heart could smell roasting potatoes and steaming cider.

Then, beyond the laughing people and the shouting children, she noticed a painted wagon.

"Binney!" she breathed. "The Gypsies are here!"

She closed the door, hope growing inside her.

The people of Castle Avamir were dressed like nobles; the women's dresses were colored like spring flowers.

"I know what to do," Heart said slowly, "but we have to hurry."

She explained, waiting for someone to tell her it was too dangerous. Instead Terrin hugged her tightly. "That's so clever!"

"You girls first," one of the women said.

Terrin and Leah stepped forward.

Heart peeked out. The ball game had gotten exciting. The women were calling back and forth, laughing.

The people at the bonfire were singing.

No one was looking toward the castle.

Heart nodded. "Go straight to the Gypsies and explain everything to Binney."

Smiling nervously, Leah and Terrin slipped through the door.

Heart watched through the crack.

The girls walked slowly, talking.

"Perfect," Heart said.

She heard the people behind her sigh in relief.

When Heart saw Terrin and Leah reach the

Gypsy wagons, she let three more girls step out the door.

The Gypsies began to light their lanterns.

Zim was shouting, talking to the crowd.

Heart heard a dog bark. Kip! And Avamir had to be there too! Heart felt dizzy with joy. If Ruth was all right and everyone could get to safety . . .

Flute music brought her thoughts to a standstill.

Zim was playing.

Heart smiled. "They're starting their show."

Heart peeked out, then opened the door just wide enough for two women and two men to slide out into the gray light of the morning.

Six went the next time, while Kip was barking and doing tricks with Sadie and Talia.

Within minutes, the people from Castle Avamir had sifted into the crowds on the grass, walking in the cool morning air.

Heart left last.

Silk and lace sleeves swayed as the nobles applauded Davey's juggling. Binney had set the lanterns in a circle that put the crowd's backs toward the secret door.

Beyond them, Heart saw the people of Castle Avamir drifting toward the trees on the far side.

In moments they would be gone, hidden by the forest.

"Heart!"

She turned to see Binney and ran to hug her.

Kip ran in happy circles around them, barking.

"We have missed you so, Heart," Binney murmured. "Where is Moonsilver?"

Heart gestured toward the forest. "Waiting."

"Will he stay where you left him?"

Heart nodded. "He will. He understands everything."

"Avamir is like that," Binney laughed. "I tell her my worries sometimes."

Davey ran up, carrying his juggling clubs. He kissed Heart's cheek. "Is Moonsilver safe?"

Heart nodded.

"The boy lord is here, Heart," Davey whispered. "Lord Irmaedith. His horse has armor your friend

Tibbs made." Davey leaned closer. "He asked me if we had seen you."

Heart flushed.

"Most of your folks are in the woods now," Binney was saying. "Zim will play for Avamir's act and . . ." She turned to Heart. "Do you have your flute?"

Heart nodded.

"Borrow a skirt from Talia and you can earn your keep!" Davey teased, then he ran off.

Heart changed into Talia's long, blue skirt, then unrolled her bundle. She couldn't wait to show Binney and Ruth her baby blanket. She took out her flute, then touched the carved unicorn horn.

It was light enough, she was sure.

Maybe she could use the pine gum to glue it to Avamir's forehead instead of the goat horn?

It would certainly look more real.

Heart slid the horn into the skirt's pocket.

Then she repacked her carry-sack and ran. When Avamir saw her coming, she arched her neck, then galloped toward Heart.

Heart kissed her, careful of the sticky pine gum.

"I love you," Heart whispered.

Avamir rested her muzzle on Heart's head, breathing in the scent of her hair.

Heart finally stepped back. She took out the carved horn.

"Would you rather have this? It might be too heavy but—"

Avamir tossed her head. Her eyes were rimmed in white as she lashed her tail back and forth.

"Heart?" Zim called.

Heart put the horn back in her pocket, sorry she had startled Avamir.

"Heart?" It was Binney this time. "Hurry!"

Heart kissed Avamir's muzzle, then ran. In a way, this show would be the most important one the Gypsies had ever given.

The moment she was beside him, Zim began to play.

Heart lifted her flute to her lips.

Their melodies rose in the morning air.

The crowd was silent, swaying.

The people of Castle Avamir had disappeared into the woods.

Heart couldn't spot any of them.

But she played her flute for them. She played for her parents, wherever they were, for her brother, if he was alive, for Ruth and the Gypsies and all the people she loved.

Her music had never been so beautiful. The flute sang of loneliness and love and family . . . and magic.

Davey began the act.

He juggled on the high wire.

He fell and pretended to be hurt.

Avamir galloped out and circled, bending dramatically to touch her glued-on goat horn to Davey's lips.

He stood slowly, uncertainly, his face a portrait of amazement as he pretended to be healed.

The crowd applauded wildly.

They cheered.

Then another sound ran through the audience. It was a strange, uneasy sound. Heart turned to see what was the matter.

A woman screamed.

+CHAPTER ELEVEN

At first Heart saw only the tangle of horses and men, some walking, some riding.

They were coming toward the castle, straggling out of the woods.

Then she saw the stretcher. Two men carried it, their hands tight on the poles.

Heart gasped. The white hair, stained with blood—it was Lord Dunraven, gravely hurt.

Heart knew Moonsilver could heal him. But if he came down here, he would be surrounded by guards. . . .

No.

She would not trade Moonsilver's life for Lord Dunraven's.

Heart spotted Ruth, walking behind the stretcher. She carried her herb bag.

Heart ran toward her. Ruth needed to know she was safe, that the people of Castle Avamir were free—and that they all needed to leave the castle *now*.

Ruth saw her coming. Her face stiffened. She shook her head, motioning Heart away.

Heart slowed, staring. Lord Dunraven's eyes were open, but he was pale as milk.

"Catch her!" she heard him rasp. "Catch the girl!"

Heart spun around, but it was too late.

Guards grabbed her and dragged her forward.

"There is an old unicorn out there," Dunraven said as she got closer, "beyond the Sunset Gates, up the Old Road." He pulled in a ragged breath. "I knew about him. I thought he was the last one." He paused and coughed. "I meant to end them all, forever."

"Why?" Heart whispered.

Dunraven coughed again. "People who believe the stories . . . they want adventure, magic. They stop working. They don't obey the nobles."

Heart glanced at Ruth, then met Lord

Dunraven's eyes. "But the stories are true. They *are*. You saw young Lord Irmaedith, how sick he was. . . ."

Lord Dunraven closed his eyes.

He coughed again and Heart saw blood on his lips.

"Heart!" Binney shouted.

She turned.

The people of Castle Avamir were walking across the field. Their heads were down. Guards strode behind them.

Heart clenched her fists. No. She could not let this happen.

She knelt beside Lord Dunraven. "Send your men and the nobles inside. I can save your life," she whispered.

He opened his eyes.

Heart gestured at the people of Castle Avamir. "Free them. And Ruth and the old man who was in the tower with us, and the Gypsies . . . and me." She stared into Lord Dunraven's eyes. "Vow to free us all forever and I will save your life."

He grimaced and looked away.

Ruth leaned toward Heart. "His horse fell, threw him onto the rocks, child. Are you sure—"

Lord Dunraven made an angry sound, waving her to silence. Then he coughed. He nodded and gestured for a guard to bend close as he gave the orders. His voice was weak, choked.

The guards began shouting, walking through the crowds.

The stretcher-bearers set Lord Dunraven down gently.

They followed the others walking toward the castle.

The people of Castle Avamir stood uneasily in the center of the field.

"There will be stories about you, True Heart!" a voice called. Heart looked up to see Seth grinning. He waved at her. "I will see you again one day!"

Heart smiled at him, her spirits lifted by his joyous face. Then she turned to see the old gardener walking across the grass, alone.

The guards were gone.

The field was quiet.

Heart looked at Lord Dunraven.

"Promise that you will never hurt any of us again, ever, that everyone here will be free to come and go."

"I give you my word," he said slowly. "Just . . . hurry."

He sounded weaker.

"You have to open the Old Road. Let the unicorns live in their ancient lands or their castle or wherever they choose," the old man added as he came close.

Lord Dunraven nodded. "I will." His voice was barely a whisper. His skin looked faintly bluish.

Heart raised her flute to her lips. She played the old melody—the one she had made up, the one that Moonsilver had learned as a colt.

The wind carried it up the mountainside.

She knew he would come.

Heart turned to Ruth. "I have to go with the people of Castle Avamir. I want so much to find my family."

Ruth held Heart close.

Tears filled Heart's eyes.

"I love you, dear girl," Ruth told her. "I will be waiting your return."

Heart leaned back to look into Ruth's eyes. "I will come to see you. I promise." She felt the bracelet tighten, and for once she knew what it meant her to do. She pulled it off her arm and slid it over Ruth's hand.

The silver threads loosened, reweaving themselves to fit Ruth's arm perfectly. The tiny flower settled into the design.

Ruth looked astonished. Heart smiled at her.

Hoofbeats in the distance made them both turn.

Moonsilver leaped from the woods, crossing the grassy field in a long-striding, graceful gallop.

He plunged to a halt in front of Heart, his mane flying.

She reached up to embrace him.

"Heal him, Moonsilver," she said quietly, explaining Dunraven's vow. Then she stepped back and raised her voice. "Lord Dunraven has promised to let us all live free!"

The people of Castle Avamir cheered. They began dancing in circles, hands clasped like children dizzy with spring.

Moonsilver approached the stretcher.

Heart held her breath as Lord Dunraven closed his eyes.

Moonsilver lowered his head.

His long silvery horn touched Lord Dunraven's lips.

An instant later, Lord Dunraven's eyes opened. His skin darkened and flushed. He sat up. His eyes were full of wonder.

The gardener chuckled and Heart glanced at him.

Then a shout made her turn. The people of Castle Avamir were running toward Moonsilver.

He reared, then galloped to meet them. Heart saw him bend to touch Leah . . . and her whole body began to change, her outline blurring and spinning.

And then there was a beautiful unicorn standing where a girl had stood a moment before.

Lord Dunraven made a sound of disgust. A murmur of astonishment rose from the Gypsies. Binney ran across the grass, with Davey and Zim close behind her.

Amazed and confused, Heart hugged them all at once, three sets of arms around her.

Kip ran in circles around them all, barking.

"Young Lord Irmaedith called you True Heart," Binney whispered in her ear. "He's right. The truest one I know. Please come back to us now and then."

Heart nodded and wiped her eyes.

Kip jumped against her legs.

Heart knelt to let him lick her face.

Then she stood and turned, her vision still blurred with tears.

Moonsilver had touched Terrin with his horn, and she was changing, shimmering in the light of sunrise.

Heart watched Moonsilver bend his head and

touch an older woman, then one of the men.

In a few moments Leah and Terrin were galloping in wide arcs across the grass, leaping in joy.

Heart finally understood. The people of Castle Avamir didn't know about unicorns. They *were* unicorns.

They had changed themselves into people to hide from the hunters long ago. They had remained in human form to keep from being discovered.

And to save their children from a life of hiding and danger, they had given them to others to raise.

"It takes a whole unicorn to change them back and forth," Lord Dunraven said in a low voice. "Once I had the mare's horn, if I had captured that old stallion, if he had truly been the last one . . ."

"They would have had to remain people forever," Heart said.

Lord Dunraven nodded. "It would have been the end of them."

Heart watched, astonished, as another woman became a lovely white unicorn, then two more of the men were changed.

Moonsilver touched them all, carefully, somberly.

It was clear he felt the weight of his responsibility.

Then he turned, cantering toward her. Avamir galloped to join him.

"I think," the gardener said, "that your little brother and your mother would like you to go home with them now."

Heart turned, trying to absorb what he had said.

"You have a large family," the old man added. "Some might not wish to change back." He gestured at Ruth, then at Binney. "But they are your family nonetheless."

Heart blinked back more tears. Then Moonsilver was close, rearing, sliding to a halt. Avamir was beside her too, lowering her head.

Heart pulled the horn out of her pocket.

"Put it where it belongs," the old man said.

Trembling, Heart raised the horn to Avamir's forehead.

Moonsilver touched it gently.

There was a brilliant light, as though five suns had risen.

Heart blinked.

Then the horn was silvery, whole, and Avamir's scars were gone. Her mane and tail were no longer white.

They were silver, shining in the early sunlight.

Heart turned to Lord Dunraven. "You must keep your word."

He scowled. "I will."

The old man laughed. "He wouldn't dare break a promise to a unicorn."

Heart smiled. "I will come back. I will visit you all," she shouted.

The Gypsies cheered as she lifted her arms and closed her eyes.

Moonsilver's horn was cold against her lips.

It was the strangest moment.

Heart felt like a candle in the dark of winter.

She burned and shivered all at once.

Her hooves were light, graceful, her long mane brushed her shoulders when she reared.

She was grateful for the magic that had saved her life, all their lives.

She would use it to visit Ruth and Seth and Tibbs. . . .

She touched Binney's cheek, then Ruth's.

Davey had Kip in his arms.

Heart reared, tossing her mane.

Then she galloped after her family.

As she thundered through the Sunset Gates with the others, she saw the stark, beautiful Mountains of the Moon in the distance.

She understood the dreams she'd had all her life.

Dreams of her home.

She leaped over logs and boulders for the pure joy of doing it.

Joy.

Heart had a big family, a wonderful family who loved her as much as she loved them. And now she was finally going home.

ᛏᚺᛖ
UNICORN'S SECRET

Experience the Magic

When the battered mare Heart Trilby takes in presents her with a silvery white foal, Heart's life is transformed into one of danger, wonder, and miracles beyond her wildest imaginings. Read about Heart's thrilling quest in

ALADDIN PAPERBACKS
Simon & Schuster Children's Publishing Division • www.SimonSaysKids.com

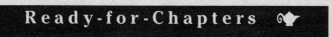

Ready-for-Chapters